When Mommy Got Cancer
Creating JOY Together

HIBISCUS PUBLISHING
About Books for Children

3611 Woodridge Place, Palm Harbor, FL. 34684

When Mommy Got Cancer—Creating JOY Together

Garcia, Karen, [04-14-68 - 01-27-11]
Illustrated by Lisa J. Michaels
Edited by Ruth E. Clark

First Edition
ISBN 13: 978-0-9842831-9-4

Printed and bound in the United States of America
by BookMasters, Inc., Ashland, OH
M10756 September 1, 2013

Summary: This is a child's story of delight in her mother's laughter – her favorite sound. This is a story of the impact her mother's illness with cancer made when it took away her favorite sound. This is a child's story of love, coping, and her search for lost laughter as the answer to the emotions and pain of cancer.

This is a story of hope, discovery, and inspiration. This is a story of a mother's love focused solely upon "being present," and upon making each precious mother-child moment together a treasure of memories to be translated into a legacy of JOY for the child she knows she must leave behind. A little child teaches life's lessons and their meaning found through Creating JOY Together.

[1.Self-Help/Motivational & Inspirational-Fiction   2.Family & Relationships/Death, Grief, Bereavement-Fiction   3.Family/General-Fiction   4.Health & Fitness/Diseases/ Cancer] I. Title
2013934441

Publisher's Preface

Sometimes there happens a special day of unannounced importance, when you sense a feeling of a tap on the shoulder intended to jar your attention to be open to receive a message of meaningful connection. One such special day, the tap on my shoulder, and the message I was meant to receive, occurred October 15th, 2010.

On that day, I was given my connection to Karen Garcia.

The envelope contained a one and one-half page introductory letter, a bio sheet two paragraphs in length, and a copy of a manuscript lovingly titled *When Mommy Got Cancer—Creating Joy Together*.

There followed an e-mail to Karen with pertinent questions November 4th; a phone conversation November 6th about exchanges of mutual diagnoses of cancer, survival status, and expressions of the shared credo of JOY; and, a November 8th letter: "Dear Karen, your manuscript has potential but requires a good deal of work. A Publisher's Critique and Outline are included." Dr. Ruth, Rx: EnJOY."

A late December e-mail informed that Karen's health was deteriorating. She would be unable to do rewrites. December 28th: "Dear Karen, Hibiscus Publishing will include your manuscript on our Project Schedule for publication." December 29th e-mail: "Dear Karen, You and I have made a connection—a connection has no boundaries. You have entrusted your dream to me. I will nurture it caringly to reality." Karen's final phone call of quiet "thank you" came a few days later.

Three e-mails, three letters, and two phone conversations have, indeed, made one meaningful connection. I am blessed to extend that connection to you with this little book. May you find caring, hope, courage, and inspiration on every page.

I invite you to **Reach for the JOY—JOY is the answer.**

—Ruth E. Clark, Ed. D.

for

Zaiden Victoria

Always my Angel Baby

When Mommy Got Cancer

Creating JOY Together

by Karen Garcia

Illustrated by Lisa J. Michaels

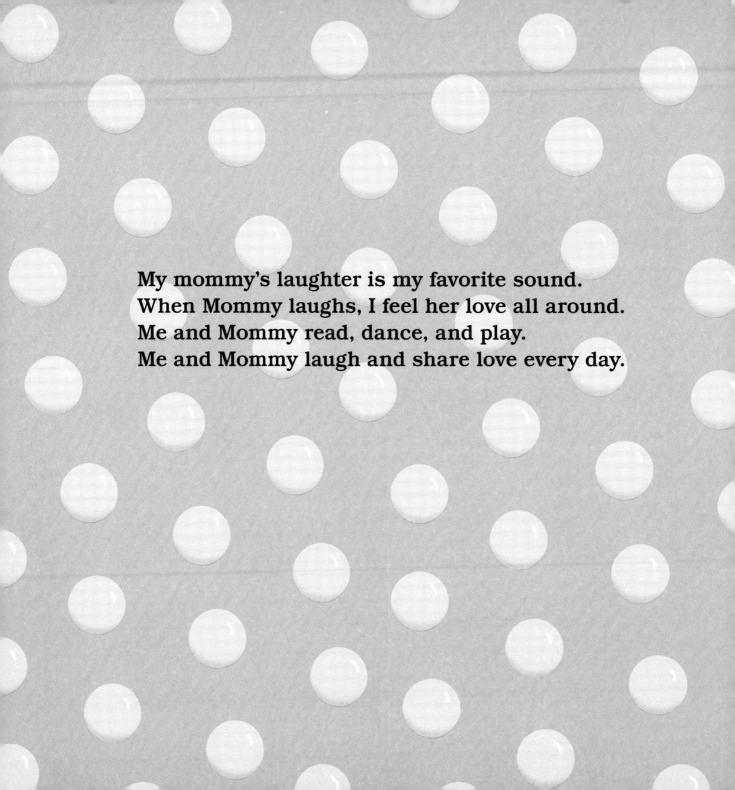

My mommy's laughter is my favorite sound.
When Mommy laughs, I feel her love all around.
Me and Mommy read, dance, and play.
Me and Mommy laugh and share love every day.

Then—
Mommy got sick.
Mommy didn't laugh anymore.
Mommy was sad. She hurt.
We couldn't play as before.

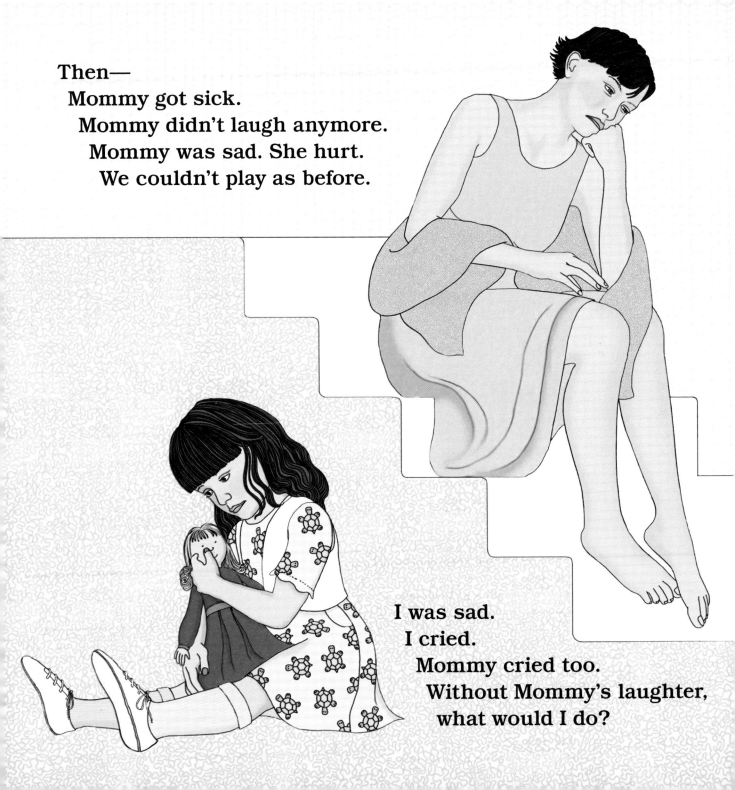

I was sad.
I cried.
Mommy cried too.
Without Mommy's laughter,
what would I do?

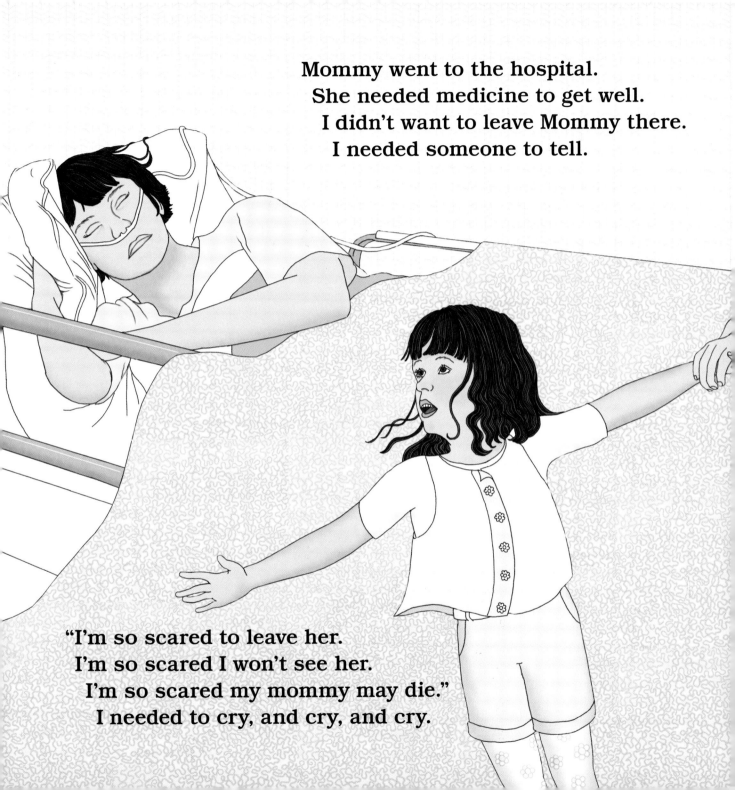

Mommy went to the hospital.
She needed medicine to get well.
I didn't want to leave Mommy there.
I needed someone to tell.

"I'm so scared to leave her.
I'm so scared I won't see her.
I'm so scared my mommy may die."
I needed to cry, and cry, and cry.

I cried.

I sobbed.

I screamed.

Why didn't
everybody see?
I needed my
Mommy at home
to play and laugh
with me.

Mommy came home.
Mommy took her rest.
Mommy took her medicine.
I behaved at my best.

I wished Mommy would laugh
  again with me.
I wished I wouldn't cry.
I needed to find happy medicine.
I really needed to try.

I used happy-colored markers
  and wrote Mommy a letter.

I read my books.
I quietly sang.
I drew.
Every day I asked God
to show me what to do.

"I'm just a child, God.
What can I do?
If I can find Mommy's laughter,
I may find the answer.
Please help Mommy laugh again,
even if she has cancer."

Mommy wore pretty
scarves, big hats,
and a wig.
We tried
them on
together.
I felt so big.

The medicine made Mommy's hair fall out.
I said she looked like a kiwi.
"Is that my new self?" Mommy laughed.
"Yes, it must be."

To me, Mommy
was her old self—
laughing again
with me.

Little by little,
Mommy's hurts
seemed to go away.
I took my guitar
and began to play.

"You look like a Rock Star!" laughed Mommy one day.

I told Mommy funny stories.
I sang her happy songs.

I jumped,
and leaped,
and ran about.

"Reach for the JOY!"

I heard Mommy shout.

I reached up.

I danced round,

and round, and round.

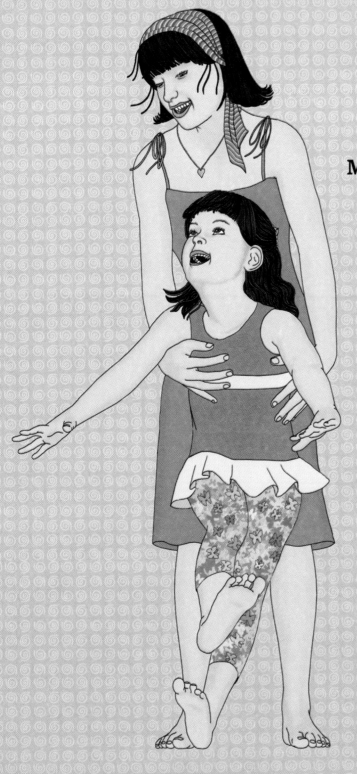

Mommy caught me when
I stopped spinning around.

Then—
I heard Mommy's laughter,
my favorite sound.

Mommy told me to tell people with cancer,
"Reach for the JOY—JOY is the answer.
Create JOY together—that is life's key."
Reaching for JOY helped Mommy and me.

Mommy's cancer didn't go away.
Mommy held me and said,
"One day, I shall leave you.
We both shall be sad.
Save in your heart, my angel girl,
all of the JOY we've had.

Then—Mommy held me.
She said, "I love you so."
Mommy kissed me goodbye.
"My darling child, I wish you to know;
I shall watch you from a cloud
as you blossom and grow."

Now—
Each day, I remember to "Reach for the JOY!"
as Mommy said.
Each night, I say our special prayer
before getting into bed.

"Thank you for matching Mommy and me.

Thank you for keeping us strong.

Thank you for our time together,
though it wasn't very long.

Thank you for the JOY
Mommy and me found.

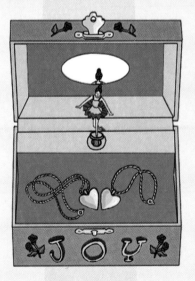

Thank you for Mommy's laughter,
my favorite sound."

The End of my story—
The Staging of my JOYful life.

■ About the Author:

Karen Ann Puanani Garcia was born in Honolulu, Hawaii. Karen attended high school in Montclair, New Jersey and went on to Rutgers University, Mason Gross Acting School. She pursued her passion for acting through a career in New York City and Los Angeles.

Karen's daughter, Zaiden Victoria, was born in November 2004; and, Karen turned her passion to expressions of unconditional love and caring in her new role as mother.

In 2007, Karen was diagnosed with Stage IV breast cancer.

Karen chronicled her search for life's meaning and documented the milestones in her struggle for survival by writing passages of truth, honesty, faith, love, and inspiration. Karen found JOY through her short time as "the mom Zaiden had chosen;" committing to being present in every moment they shared. Karen took her final bow and exited this life's stage in her 43rd year on January 27th, 2011.

Karen wrote the manuscript for *When Mommy Got Cancer—Creating Joy Together* as her legacy of hope, inspiration, and JOY. This book represents the realization of Karen's wish and intent to continue to "be present for Zaiden, my Angel Baby."

■ About the Illustrator:

Lisa J. Michaels is a professional illustrator and a member of the Society of Children's Book Writers & Illustrators since 2003. Lisa is the creator and developer of: The Visual Storyteller's Studio (www.theVSS.org), The Yellow Brick Road, and of The SCBWI West Coast Critters, the official SCBWI on-line illustrator critique group of Florida.

Lisa's portfolio and resume can be viewed at her personal website, www.ljmichaels-illustrator.com. Contact: ljmillustrations@yahoo.com

■ About the Editor and Publisher:

Ruth E. Clark, Ed. D. is an educator serving families and children with special needs.

Dr. Clark is a breast cancer survivor and has committed to "Choose JOY."

Dr. Clark founded Hibiscus Publishing—About Books for Children in 2007; and has since authored and published six award-winning children's picture books.

Read to Someone You Love was founded as the service arm for Hibiscus Publishing with a mission to contribute to charities for children and to non-profit organizations promoting cancer awareness and programs for survivor support. Dr. Clark participates in author reading/guest programs in children's hospitals, schools, and libraries. She enjoys a speaking circuit for fund-raising events. Contact: hibiscus311@verizon.net.